Winnie the Pooh

Pooh's Wishful Thinking

Today is a not-so-special, very special day in the Hundred-Acre Wood. Christopher Robin invites everyone to join him for a picnic.

"I wished that today would be a perfect day for a picnic," says Christopher Robin, "and look—my wish came true!"

Everyone cheers, "Hooray for picnics! Hooray for perfect days! Hooray for wishes!"

Winnie the Pooh is think-think-thinking. He is thinking about Christopher Robin, and the wish he made.

"I was just thinking that I don't remember if I have ever made a wish," says Pooh. "And I don't suppose I know what I would wish for if I did make one—a wish, that is."

But everyone has wishes in the Hundred-Acre Wood. Christopher Robin asks his friends to help Pooh. "Let's share with Pooh Bear the wishes we have wished," says Christopher Robin.

Rabbit says he once wished for help in his garden. He was very busy, and gardening was too much work for one rabbit to do.

"Did your wish come true?" asks Pooh.

Well, all of Rabbit's friends did come to help. But Rabbit thought Tigger bounced too much, so he made a second wish. He wished Tigger would bounce in a different part of the Hundred-Acre Wood.

Piglet once wished he could play a game with his friends.

"What game did you wish to play?" asks Pooh.

"Hide and seek," says Piglet.

All of Piglet's friends laugh. You see, Piglet always wins at "Hide and seek." He is a very small animal, and very small animals can hide almost anywhere.

"I, too, had a wish," says Owl. "I wished to glow like the fireflies of the night."

"Why would you wish that?" asks Pooh.

"Because then you could see me when I fly at night, just as I see you," says Owl.

"Did your wish come true?" asks Pooh.

"Sadly, no," replies Owl.

"Well, I'm rather glad," says Pooh. "I like you just the way you are."

Eeyore also had a wish. He wished his face wasn't so squiggly. "If my face wasn't so squiggly, I could see it better," explained Eeyore.

But it was not Eeyore's face that was squiggly. It was his ears that made the ripples in the water, and that made his face look squiggly-wiggly.

Eeyore thanks Pooh for noticing.

Pooh thanks Eeyore for sharing his wish.

Tigger once wished everybody could bounce just like him. "Bouncing's what tiggers do best!" he said.

But not all things are meant to bounce. Some things fly, and other things crawl. Some things swim, and other things wiggle. That's what they do best!

Pooh decides not to wish Tigger's wish. He likes all the different things his animal friends can do.

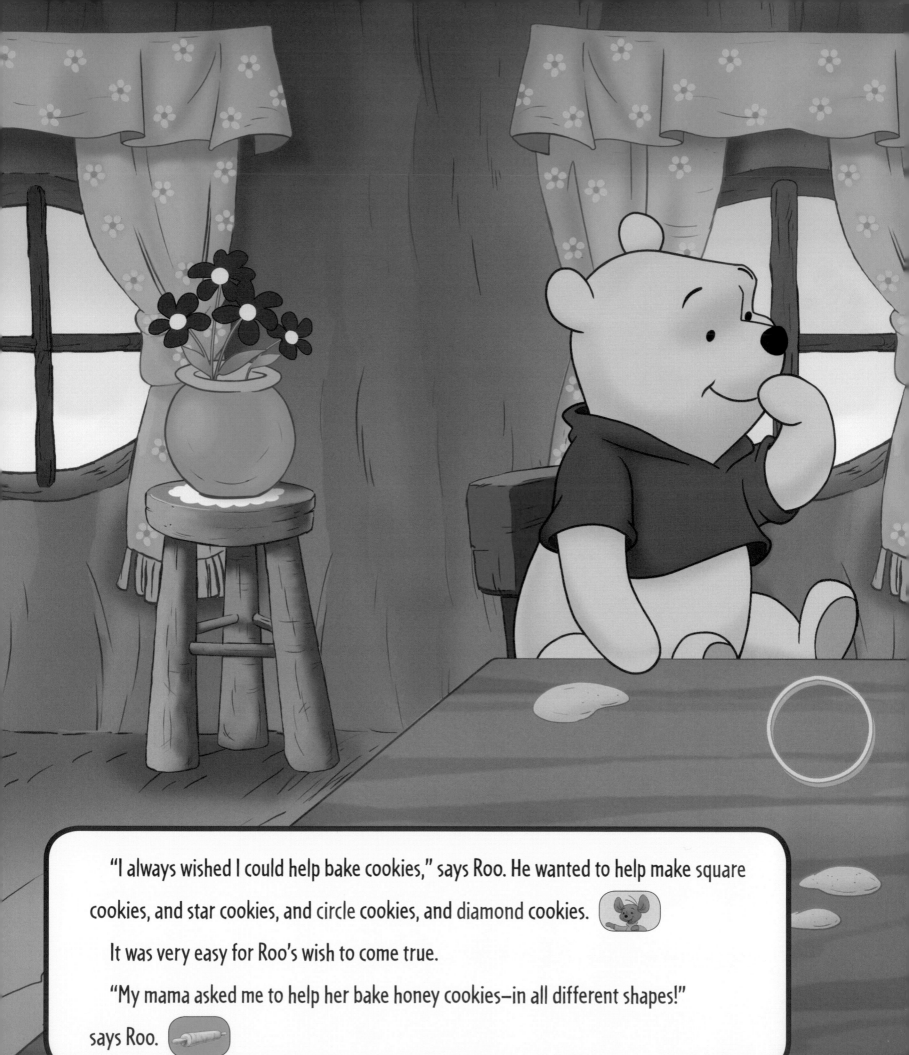

"I always wished I could help bake cookies," says Roo. He wanted to help make square cookies, and star cookies, and circle cookies, and diamond cookies.

It was very easy for Roo's wish to come true.

"My mama asked me to help her bake honey cookies—in all different shapes!" says Roo.

Kanga was happy to help Roo's wish come true.

First, they got all the tools and ingredients ready. Second, they poured the ingredients into a bowl. Third, they mixed the ingredients up. (That was messy!) Fourth, they shaped the dough into cookies. Fifth, they put the soft dough into the hot oven. Last, they pulled the fresh honey cookies out of the oven!

Mmmmm! Pooh likes Roo's wish most of all.

"You see, Pooh, wishes are hopes you have between yourself and you," Christopher Robin says. "And everybody is full of wishes. Do you understand?"

"Yes, I believe I do," says Pooh.

"Would you like to make a wish right now, Pooh?" asks Piglet.

"Yes, I believe I would," says Pooh.

Pooh could wish for a surprise rainbow.

"I like colors," says Pooh.

Which one is his favorite? Well, red is the color of Pooh's shirt. Yellow is like honey. Orange makes him think of Tigger. Roo's shirt is blue. Green is the color of grass. And purple looks like the flowers of the woods.

"I like them all," says Pooh. But he does not wish for a surprise rainbow.

Pooh could wish for wings. Then he would flutter and fly, like the bees.

"I'll use my wings to get to the honey that's up high in the tree," says Pooh.

"But, Pooh," replies Piglet, "if you flap your arms to fly, what will you use to grab the honey?"

"Oh, bother," says Pooh. He does not wish for wings, either.

At last, Pooh knows what his wish will be. He closes his eyes, counts to three, and wishes that all his favorite friends would spend the day with him.

"Silly old bear!" says Christopher Robin. "You've already got your wish."

Sure enough, Pooh's friends are all around him, ready for the picnic.

"And I got my wish, again," says Roo. He helped Kanga bake cookies for everyone!

At night, Christopher Robin and Pooh rest near Pooh's Thoughtful Spot.

"Would you like to make a wish on a star?" asks Christopher Robin.

"Can I?" replies Pooh.

"Of course," says Christopher Robin.

"On all of them?" asks Pooh.

"Yes, Pooh Bear," says Christopher Robin.

"Then I shall wish for one honeypot on each star in the sky," says Pooh.